Mermaid KINGDOM

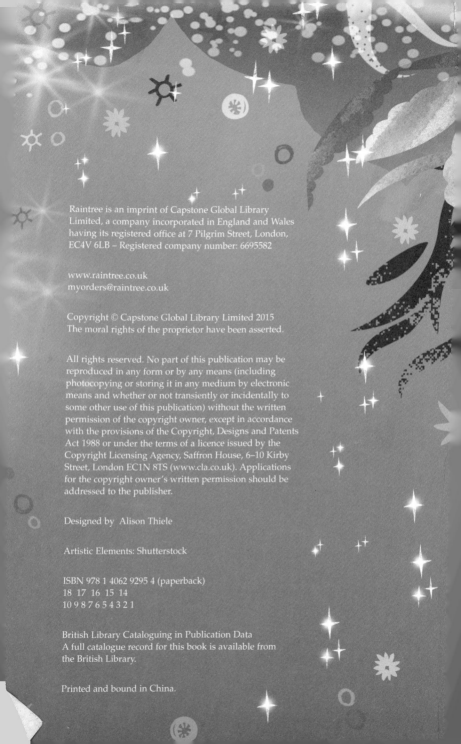

Raintree is an imprint of Capstone Global Library
Limited, a company incorporated in England and Wales
having its registered office at 7 Pilgrim Street, London,
EC4V 6LB – Registered company number: 6695582

www.raintree.co.uk
myorders@raintree.co.uk

Designed by Alison Thiele

Artistic Elements: Shutterstock

ISBN 978 1 4062 9295 4 (paperback)
18 17 16 15 14
10 9 8 7 6 5 4 3 2 1

British Library Cataloguing in Publication Data
A full catalogue record for this book is available from
the British Library.

Printed and bound in China.

Cora's Decision

by Janet Gurtler

illustrated by Katie Wood

raintree 🍃

a Capstone company — publishers for children

Mermaid life

✦ Mermaid Kingdom refers to all the
kingdoms in the sea, including Neptunia,
Caspian, Hercules, Titania and Nessland.
Each kingdom has a King and Queen who
live in a castle. Merpeople live in caves.

✦ Mermaids get their legs on their thirteenth
birthdays at the stroke of midnight. It's a
celebration when the mermaid makes her
first voyage onto land. After their thirteenth
birthdays, mermaids can go onto land for short
periods of time but must be very careful.

✦ If a mermaid goes onto land before her
thirteenth birthday, she will get her legs early
and never get her tail back. She will lose all
memories of being a mermaid and will be
human forever.

☆ Mermaids are able to stay on land with legs for no more than forty-eight hours. Any longer and they will not be able to get their tails back and will be human forever. They will lose all memories of being a mermaid.

☆ If they fall in love, merpeople and humans can marry and have babies (with special permission from the King and Queen of their kingdom). Their babies are half-human and half-merperson. However, this love must be the strongest love possible in order for it to be approved by the King and Queen.

☆ Half-human mermaids are able to go on land indefinitely and can change back into a mermaid at any point. However, they are not allowed to tell other humans about the mermaid world unless they have special permission from the King and Queen.

Chapter one

It didn't matter how much fun the summer holidays had been. The first day back at school was always really exciting. Of course, I was nervous about school starting again. But I was more excited than nervous.

I couldn't wait to find out which teacher I would have. I was hoping that my best friends Rachel and Shyanna would be in the same class as me. I could survive without them, but it definitely wouldn't be as much fun. When school started, I wouldn't have to look after my sisters all day, which was a huge bonus.

Plus, this was a big year for me. It was the first year I'd be able to audition for the special mermaid dance group. The dance group is an important part of each kingdom. They attend school and community events, bringing a fun dynamic through dancing, singing and cheering. Once you are on the team, you are a part of it for life!

I'd dreamed about being on the team since I was a baby, when Mum would tell me stories about being on the team. These days, my mum was so busy with my sisters that sometimes it felt like she'd forgotten about me. Being on the special mermaid dance group would definitely make her notice me!

On the morning of the first day of school, my little sisters helped me decide what to wear. I couldn't decide which top screamed special mermaid dance group the most. I narrowed it down to a new purple one and my favourite light blue one. When I came out of the bathroom in my new purple top, my sisters clapped and squealed. It was clearly the winner.

Sometimes I complained about how loud my sisters were, but I liked having them around when I needed a cheering section. They really could be sweet sometimes.

"Cora! Rachel and Shyanna are here," my mum called to me.

"Just in time," I said.

"Bye, Cora! Have fun! Good luck with your lessons!" my mum shouted as she tucked Jewel under one arm and chased Pearl and Ruby through the hallway. Sweet or not, those girls were a lot of work!

"Bye!" I called to my sisters and my mum, even though I knew they weren't listening.

"Wow!" Shyanna said. "That purple top really suits you!"

"Thanks." We raved about each other's outfits. I admired Rachel's curly red hair and Shyanna's plaits. The three of us linked arms and started swimming towards school. Luckily I lived fairly close, which is why we all met up at my cave.

"I'm really nervous," Rachel said as we approached the front of the school. I wasn't surprised that Rachel was nervous. She moved to Neptunia over the summer holiday, and being the new girl was hard. Plus, it made me feel better that I wasn't the only nervous one.

"Don't worry, we've got your tail," Shyanna said.

"It's my legs I'm more worried about," Rachel joked, trying to relieve some tension.

Rachel was half-human, which was a big secret. She didn't want any of the children to find out and bully her. She'd had some problems at her old school, so it made sense that she would hide her secret.

Shy and I were so excited about catching up with our school friends and introducing them to Rachel. We knew they were going to love her as much as we did. We arrived at school and stopped to admire the giant statue of the school's founding mermaid, Michelle, at the school's entrance. We showed Rachel how to rub Michelle's fin for luck.

"Everyone's going to love you just the way you are," I said. I didn't think anyone would care that she was half-human, except maybe to think it was really cool that she could go onto land whenever she wanted and for as long as she wanted.

We swam together through the pillars of old white coral that led into the school grounds. It was chaotic inside. Merboys and mergirls of all ages were doing flips and mingling and waving to each other.

"Hi!" I shouted to Cassie Shores as she swam by with a group of mergirls. She was one of the most popular mermaids at school and was also on the swimming team with me last year. Like me, she was excited that this year we were eligible to audition for the special mermaid dance group.

"She's a shoo-in for the dance group," I told Rachel. "She composes songs, and she's amazing at it. Getting a place on the special mermaid dance group will be a great way for you to get to know her too!"

"Cool," Rachel said. "If you like her, so will I."

"She's as obsessed as Cora about being on the special mermaid dance group," Shyanna said.

"I wouldn't say obsessed," Cora said.

"I would!" Shyanna winked to let me know it was okay, but Rachel wasn't paying any attention. Instead, she was looking at a group of mermaids swimming by.

"That's the girl who said things about my mum during the Royal Concert," Rachel whispered to us.

"That's Regina," Shyanna said. "She's not the nicest mermaid."

"That is a huge understatement! She is just nasty," I said as I glanced at Regina and frowned.

I needed to show positive behaviour because the dance group selections were coming up, but it wasn't always easy.

Chapter two

I didn't have long to dwell on Regina and her nastiness because our headteacher's voice boomed over the PA system. "Attention, everyone. Please report to the Dolphin Sports Hall. We are ready to announce the class lists for this school year. Also, we have a special surprise this morning."

A special surprise? That sounded like a fantastic way to start the school year!

We joined the crowd of merkids swimming into the hall. Everyone was whispering and pointing, and

I certainly understood why when I saw who was on the stage.

"That's the King and Queen!" Shyanna whispered, though it was quite obvious. They were wearing crowns and were so regal looking with their shiny hair and sparkling tails. They were a beautiful couple!

Our headteacher stood on the stage. "Welcome back, everyone! Before the King and Queen make their special announcement, I am going to read out the class lists for this year. Please settle down and listen closely."

It took a couple of minutes to get all the merkids organized. Rachel, Shyanna and I stuck together. Rachel was gripping our hands so tightly it hurt. She was also looking a little panicked. Because she was new at school, she was a little bit nervous about everything. I smiled to show her that we were all in this together.

As our headteacher read name after name, I was getting even more hopeful that the three of us would be in the same class together. And guess what? That's exactly what happened! Shyanna, Rachel and I were in Ms Swift's class together!

Once the excitement of class lists died down, our headteacher announced the King and Queen. The entire crowd went quiet as the pair stood and moved to the front of the stage.

"As you all know, this is the one-hundredth anniversary of Mermaid Kingdom," the King said. "To celebrate, there will be a Mermaid Kingdom Festival, including a special competition between individual kingdoms."

"Merkids from each kingdom will form teams to compete in a series of special spirit competitions, including singing, dancing and chanting or cheering," the Queen announced. "We want to wish the merkids of Neptunia good luck!"

"The team that shows the best teamwork throughout the competition will win a trophy and a big donation for their kingdom and school," the King added.

A cheer rose from the merkids gathered in the hall. I couldn't believe this was happening! As it was the one-hundredth anniversary of Mermaid Kingdom, being on the special mermaid dance group was even more important than ever!

The Queen raised her hand again. "Earlier today, we picked the team leader for Neptunia. Based on community involvement and outstanding school achievements, Regina Merrick is your team leader."

As Regina, with a smug look on her face, confidently waved at everyone, there were polite claps. There were more groans than cheers.

I was really hoping Cassie would get to be the team leader, as she was nice, fair and talented. There wasn't anything I could do about it now but politely clap and deal with it.

The headteacher congratulated Regina, thanked the Queen and King for their appearance, and dismissed us to our classrooms. The chaos and noise quickly returned as we swam out of the hall.

"Are you nervous about auditioning for the dance group?" I asked Rachel.

She bit her lip and nodded. "I don't think Regina likes me very much."

"Regina doesn't like many people," Shyanna said.

"Don't worry about her!" I said with a smile. "With your voice, you're perfect for the team! You may be new, but you've already been noticed."

Shyanna looked at me and then back at Rachel. "Maybe Rachel doesn't want to be on the Neptunia Special mermaid dance group," she said.

"What? That's crazy!" I said. I couldn't even imagine not wanting to be on the team.

"That's not it. I'm just nervous," Rachel said.

"Me too!" I said.

"I don't know why you're so nervous, Cora," Shyanna said. "You are really athletic and everyone likes you. Plus, you have a great attitude about everything, which is rare."

"Thank you, Shy," I said, blushing a little.

"You're perfect for the Neptunia team, just like your mum was," Shyanna said as she turned to Rachel. "Cora's mum was on the Neptunia dance group for the seventy-fifth anniversary of Mermaid Kingdom. She helped bring the trophy to Neptunia."

"I want to start practising straight away," I said. "Can we rehearse at your cave, Rachel? My sisters will be in the way at mine."

"Of course!" Rachel said. "Maybe my dad can even help us with a new song."

"Fantastic! We really can't get better help than the Queen's music teacher!" I said.

"You see? Just because Regina is in charge it doesn't mean we can't have fun, does it?" Shyanna said.

I nodded, thankful. What would I do without my friends?

Chapter three

By the end of the week, I was in full school mode. The school year was going really well. I loved Ms Swift. We were studying shipwrecks in sea studies, and we even went on a field trip to explore an old sunken ship. Ms Swift always let Rachel and Shyanna and me work together. The only thing that made my heart sink was that Rachel seemed so different at school. She was so quiet and reserved. Shyanna and I did everything we could to involve her, but it didn't help.

There was nothing wrong with being shy, but that wasn't the real Rachel. When she was with me and Shyanna alone, she was so full of spark and energy. But at school, she was so worried about the other mermaids finding out her secret that she barely talked at all.

Rachel thought the merkids wouldn't want to be friends with her if they knew she was half-human. I knew Cassie and her group of friends would accept Rachel no matter what. They were nice girls. I told Rachel she should announce it at the top of her lungs, but Shyanna explained to me that Rachel needed to do things her own way.

I had to stop focusing on Rachel and focus on the auditions for the special mermaid dance group. My plan was to rehearse every day after school, but getting together with Shyanna and Rachel was harder than breaking open an oyster shell.

Because of the special anniversary this year, the auditions were less than a week away. They wanted to give the special mermaid dance group more time to rehearse as a team.

Every time Rachel, Shyanna and I organized an after-school rehearsal, there seemed to be some sort of family emergency.

First, Pearl became unwell and I had to look after Jewel and Ruby while my mum took Pearl to the doctor. Then, Jewel ripped her tail and needed stitches, so I had to babysit again. Just when everything seemed fine, Ruby got the flu and Mum made me stay at home and help. Those three girls were such a handful!

I often envied the quietness of being an only child, like Shyanna and Rachel. The two of them were practising a lot at Rachel's, and they didn't even need to.

I hated missing the rehearsals with the girls. I also hated missing out on the fun. Besides, Rachel's dad was the Queen's singing coach. Rachel's dad was the Queen's singing teacher.

Fortunately, my sisters, my cousin Shelby, and my parents liked to watch me perform. They helped by singing Rachel and Shyanna's parts when I was rehearsing.

I knew my moves, but I still wasn't confident about my singing. I knew Rachel and Shyanna would make it into the special mermaid dance group because their voices were so amazing. My plan was to distract the judges from my singing voice by dancing my heart out. I could sing, but it wasn't my best talent. I could do good harmonies, but I wasn't a power singer like my friends.

But that wasn't going to stop me. I wasn't going to let anything stand in the way of making it into the dance group. I had been dreaming about this for too long to give up. All I could do was work hard and try my best. That had to count for something, didn't it?

Chapter four

Finally, the day for the audition arrived. Rachel, Shyanna and I wore matching pink tops and pink nail varnish. Shy's mum even made us matching sea flower tiaras.

Before our performance, the three of us put our heads together. "Let's do this, girls!" I squealed. We swished our tails together, and then the music for our routine started.

What happened next was a bit of a blur. I know I hit all of my notes, and Shyanna and Rachel sang like angels. As for the dancing, we nailed it! We were in perfect unison, and each solo was unique and energetic.

Afterwards, I was so relieved it was over that I could barely talk. We stayed to watch the other performers. I was impressed. Everyone did an incredible job, and with that kind of competition, I knew it was going to be tough to make it onto the team.

When all the performers had finished, our headteacher announced that the judges would go and vote. The judges were former members of the Special mermaid dance group. Because Regina was the team leader, she got to make all the final decisions.

I bit all the glittery nail varnish off of my nails whilst we waited for the committee to return with the results. The water in the hall seemed electric, and everyone was bursting with excitement. Finally the committee members swam back inside, led by Regina. I felt positively seasick.

"Don't worry, Cora," Rachel whispered calmly. "You're going to make it onto the team. I know it."

My pulse was racing. Shyanna took my other hand as Regina stepped forwards. She smiled with her pearly white teeth.

Rachel took a deep, nervous breath. It was my turn to squeeze her hand. "You were great," I whispered to her.

Rachel nodded, but her lips were one thin line again. She looked a little pale as well.

"The results are in," the headteacher announced. "The special mermaid dance group members have been selected. Thank you to every mermaid and merboy who auditioned. Your obvious talents made the decision particularly difficult, which is a nice problem to have. And now, I will hand things over to Regina. Regina, you may do the honor."

"Thank you. The first member of the special

mermaid dance group," Regina announced, "is Shyanna Angler."

Everyone went mad clapping and cheering. I screamed so loudly that I nearly passed out. Shyanna grinned and swam to the front. A few more names were called; most of them were mermaids I knew and had been positive would make it onto the team.

Regina announced a few more names, including Cassie. We all cheered extra loudly for her. No matter how much I wanted to make it onto the squad, I knew Cassie wanted it just as much.

I closed my eyes and refused to count how many places were left. Instead, I started making promises inside my head. If I made it onto the team, I would never complain about my sisters again. I would always eat my krill and never make fun of snails racing again.

"And now," Regina dramatically shouted, "the final special mermaid dance group member." Every merkid in the hall seemed to be holding their breath.

"Last, but certainly not least, the final member of the Neptunia Special mermaid dance group is…" Regina cleared her throat and paused.

"Cora Bass."

My entire body whooshed with relief. A grin took over my face. But then I looked next to me and my grin disappeared.

Rachel.

Rachel hadn't made it onto the team.

Chapter five

It didn't make sense. The judges hadn't chosen Rachel? But she was one of the best singers, not only in Neptunia, but in the entire Mermaid Kingdom. I couldn't believe she hadn't made it onto the team!

"Don't feel sorry for me," Rachel said. "Go on up there and celebrate. You deserve this!"

She pushed me forwards, cheering the whole time. When I got to the front, Shyanna tackled me with a giant hug. We did a somersault together and stopped at exactly the same time.

When we looked out into the crowd at Rachel, she smiled brightly and gave us a big thumbs-up.

"I can't believe she didn't make it," I said to Shyanna.

"I know!" she answered. "It does not make sense. Something feels off about this entire process, and I bet Regina has something to do with it."

"I totally agree," Shyanna said, looking frustrated. "We need to get to the bottom of this, no matter what. Rachel does not deserve to be excluded."

The committee made some announcements, and then it was done. We swam back to Rachel.

"Don't feel bad for me," she told us as soon as we reached her. "I'm okay. I'm more than happy to help coach you two. I'm pretty good at coaching from watching my dad teach."

"Rachel, I have no idea why you aren't on the team," I said.

"But don't worry," Shyanna said. "We will figure it out."

We pulled her in for a group hug. When we let go, she blinked fast and smiled, but I saw a lone tear escape from her eye.

* * *

"That was a really great training session," Cassie said to me and Shyanna. It was fun spending more time with Cassie again. She was just as smart, funny and kind as I remembered.

"Well, except when Regina said she had to leave early," Shyanna said, "and you offered to take over. I thought she was going to have a temper tantrum, but you still insisted. I couldn't believe you did that."

I grinned. Shyanna didn't like conflict. As a big sister, I had lots of experience with it. "Nah. She was fine."

Cassie laughed. "Only because you didn't really give her a choice."

I shrugged. Regina could be horrible sometimes,

but I didn't let her get to me. She was just another mermaid. I didn't have time to worry about her.

"You did a really fantastic job leading our group," Shy said.

"I suppose being bossy comes naturally to me," I said.

Shyanna shook her head. "No. It's not being bossy. It's being a good leader. After Regina left and you took over, we were a completely different squad. We worked together so much better, which is what we need to do to win this thing."

"You're good at motivating, which is a big role for the team leader," Cassie chimed in.

"Thanks," I said, blushing. I tried to hide my proud smile, but my heart grew a few sizes. "Regina is a really good dancer and singer, though."

"But she isn't a very good leader," Shyanna replied, making a good point.

"She tries," I said. I didn't want to talk about it anymore, even though I sort of agreed with her that Regina wasn't always the best at leading the group.

I didn't want to admit it to anyone, even Shy, but I'd lost some of my excitement about being on the Special mermaid dance group. The fact that Rachel hadn't been selected still upset me. Not just because she was a great friend – fair was fair – but because she was a great performer. I suspected that perhaps Regina did have something against Rachel, and I needed to get to the bottom of it.

"Hey," I said. "My mum isn't expecting me to be home to look after my sisters for another hour. Let's go to Rachel's and see how she is. We've been so busy with special mermaid dance group lately that we haven't seen much of her."

"That's a great idea," Shyanna said.

"This is my cue to head home," Cassie said.

"Are you sure?" I asked. "You are more than welcome to come with us."

"I don't think Rachel would like that very much. I do understand, though," she said. "Being the new girl is hard."

"Another time," Shyanna agreed.

We each gave Cassie a hug and swam off quickly to see Rachel, swirling with excitement as we made our way over to Rachel's cave.

We swam up to the front door and rang the bell, but no one answered. We looked at each other.

"She's not at home," I said.

"I wonder where she's gone," Shyanna said.

"She's probably helping her dad. Let's wait. I bet they'll be home soon," I said, hoping I was right.

We played with some sea turtles and chased after some cute baby crabs who were playing hide-and-seek. Finally, Rachel swam into view.

"There you are! At last!" Shyanna said. "Where's your dad?"

"My dad?" she said.

"Weren't you helping him?" Shy asked.

Rachel smiled. "No. He's with the Queen. She's working on a new performance and needed his help."

She swam to her cave and waited for us to follow.

Shyanna and I exchanged a quick glance as we followed her into the living room. "So where were you?" I asked, even though I could guess.

"I went to visit Owen." She swam over and stretched out on a hammock, looking very pleased with herself.

Owen was Rachel's best friend, a human she'd met on land. He'd recently been granted magical merman powers to visit us in Mermaid Kingdom for two hours at a time, but it was easier for Rachel to visit him on land. Shyanna and I looked at each other again, and her worried expression echoed how I felt. Not that long ago, Rachel had been thinking about leaving Mermaid Kingdom to become human. What if she still wanted to?

"Why don't you bring him here?" I asked Rachel.

"I would rather go on land," she said and got up from the hammock. "Legs are restricting in the water, but they're fun on land. I'm learning how to run faster. It's pretty amazing."

"Are you sure you're okay?" I asked again. "You're not thinking about becoming human again, are you?"

Rachel shook her head. "Don't look so worried, you two. I'm fine. Really."

"We're your best friends," I said. "You can tell us anything."

"Well," she finally said, "maybe I feel a little bit left out because you two are so busy after school with rehearsals. But it's okay. I don't want you to feel guilty. I want you to do well at the Spirit Games."

We swam over and hugged her tight.

When we let go, she sniffled. "Maybe I'm a little bit scared you two are going to forget about me and things will be like they were in Caspian. I was so lonely there, and people made fun of me for being half-human. It was terrible."

"Is that when you started spending time with Owen?" Shy asked.

"Yes," Rachel said. "I don't know what I would have done without him."

"I hate the fact that the special mermaid dance group is making you feel so unhappy," I said. "It's supposed to make everyone happy, and I don't want to be a part of something that makes you miserable."

"I agree," Shyanna said. "We don't need to be a part of the Special mermaid dance group."

Rachel shook her head. "No. No way. I know how important this is to you two – especially you, Cora. I'm not letting you leave because of me. I'm fine."

"It *was* important to me, but our friendship is much more important," I said. "Anyway, we don't have any rehearsals tomorrow, so we must definitely catch up."

My phone rang then. It was my mum, telling me to come home. "We'll see you after school tomorrow, okay?" I said to Rachel.

She smiled and nodded, but the smile didn't reach her eyes. That didn't make me feel any better.

I had to fix it. I just wasn't sure how.

Chapter six

Before school the next day, Regina called a special meeting for the dance group. "The first competition will take place in ten days," she announced. "The contest will be at Caspian Castle, during the senior swimming gala. The special mermaid dance groups will perform between races. We need to win this and get off to a good start."

Everyone cheered and clapped.

"In preparation, we're going to have a special rehearsal after school today," Regina said.

My mouth dropped open. We'd promised Rachel we would be free to see her, but we really couldn't miss this rehearsal. Shy and I swam to find her and tell her the bad news.

"It's okay," Rachel said, smiling. "Don't look so guilty. It's exciting. I can't wait for the competition!"

The school day zipped past, and then the special mermaid dance group gathered in the hall for our rehearsal. We lined up and started the routine.

My flips had really improved, and everything was going fantastically, until the last part of the mermaid song. I opened my mouth to sing, but instead of a clear note, a horrible screech came out. It was so off key that everyone turned and looked at me. The music stopped playing. My face burned, and I covered my mouth with my hand. Regina put her hands on her hips and narrowed her eyes.

"Cora, what is wrong with you?" she said.

Everyone stared. My cheeks burned with humiliation, and my eyes filled with tears.

Shyanna swam close and patted my shoulder. "Don't worry about it. Just practise that note at home," she whispered. "You'll get it right."

We started again from the top. I fumbled through the song, singing really softly in case my voice cracked again. Regina did not look happy.

Shyanna and I swam home together, but after she left me to swim to her own cave, Regina swam up next to me. She must have been following us.

"Cora, you're the weakest link on our team," she said. "We don't want to lose because of you. If you don't think you can hit that note properly, it would be better for everyone if you left now."

I didn't want to let everyone down with my voice, but I wanted to be on the special mermaid dance group more than anything. I shook my head.

"I won't mess this up," I reassured her.

She glared at me and then nodded. "Please don't. We're having a full dress rehearsal tomorrow. You need to prove that you can do it."

With a flick of her tail, she swam away. I went inside my cave and immediately got swarmed by my sisters, who were arguing over a necklace of woven seaweed. I tried to shake off my gloom, but the tears came hard and fast.

Mum came into the room and swam to me. "Cora? Is everything okay?" She touched my forehead to see if I was warm. I wanted to tell her why I was upset, but she had enough to deal with, with all of my little sisters. I also didn't want her to know that the special mermaid dance group wasn't perfect.

Just then, the doorbell rang.

"I'm fine, Mum. I'm just tired," I said. I fake smiled and went to answer the door. It was Rachel!

"You spend some time with your friend," Mum said to me. "I'll look after the girls."

Rachel and I swam to my room. "Are you okay?" she asked. "I was coming home from visiting Owen and I saw you and Regina talking. It didn't look like a pleasant conversation."

I told her what Regina had said.

Rachel looked really cross. "Don't worry, Cora," she said. "I've got something that will help you."

Rachel asked my mum if I could go home with her. Mum let me go without even thinking about it. She knew something was wrong.

At her cave, Rachel dragged me inside her dad's room, which seemed a bit strange.

"Are we supposed to be in here?" I asked.

"It's okay. My dad keeps something of mine in his wardrobe, but I'm allowed to take it out or use it anytime I want to," Rachel said confidently.

She swam to the wardrobe, but I floated by the doorway. Rachel took something out and turned, hiding it behind her back. She smiled. "You're not allowed to say no."

Then she pulled out the most beautiful mermaid top I'd ever seen. It sparkled with every colour under the sea with a shimmery, magical quality. It literally took my breath away.

"I want you to wear this. It was my mum's. The Queen gave it to her as a special gift when she married my dad. It's magical."

"Really?" I said, not fully believing her. "I think I need more than magic to help me be a better singer."

"Well, it helped my mum sing as charmingly and skillfully as a fully-fledged mermaid," Rachel said. "Don't you think some magic had to be involved? She was a human!"

I stared at the shell top, completely amazed by how beautiful it was. Maybe it was magic!

"Oh, Rachel," I said, almost in shock. "I can't wear that. I'd be scared I'd ruin it or something. It's too precious."

Rachel shook her head. "You are one of the most kind and responsible mermaids I've ever met. And you and Shyanna have made my life in Neptunia incredibly wonderful. I insist that you borrow it. I have complete faith in you. The magic will give you courage to perform as well as I know you can.

You only have to believe in yourself, as much as you believe in everyone else around you."

I didn't even know what to say. Rachel was amazing! She was willing to help me and our team even though Regina hadn't selected her.

Rachel held out the top and slipped out of the room so I could try it on. When I swam out wearing it, Rachel clapped and whistled.

"Wow!" Rachel said with a huge smile on her face. "It's perfect on you. I mean it! It was meant to be worn by you. My dad will be thrilled to see you perform with it on."

"Are you sure?" I asked. I loved the top. Just the thought of wearing it made me believe I could sing better. "I feel so awful, Rachel. You're a gifted singer. You should be on the special mermaid dance group. Not me."

Rachel shook her head. "No, really. Your voice is lovely, Cora. You only have to believe in it. Plus, you have much more than a voice. Your incredible spirit shines from you all the time. It makes you the wonderful mermaid you are. It sounds cheesy, but I look up to you."

Tears slipped down my cheeks, but they were tears of happiness. I changed out of the top and held it out to Rachel. "Take it with you," she said.

"On no," I said. "I can't keep it at my cave. I'm afraid with all the chaos and my sisters around, it might accidentally get ruined. I need all the help and magic I can get!"

She laughed, but took it back and hung it in her dad's wardrobe. "I'll bring it to school tomorrow so you can wear it for your dress rehearsal."

I hugged her on my way out of her cave. "You are such a good friend," I said.

"So are you," she said. "See you tomorrow!"

I swam home with an extra flick in my tail and a huge smile on my face. With that extra bit of magic, I had all the confidence in the world!

Chapter seven

The next day at school, I put on the top before rehearsal. Rachel swam to the door of the hall and peeked inside to watch the others' reaction. The other merkids were amazed. They immediately surrounded me and raved about the shimmery, magical top. Even Regina swam over and nodded her approval, but she swam away quickly.

After the fussing was over, we ran through the singing number and my voice held the notes perfectly. The top really was magical!

When the rehearsal had finished, I had changed into my old top. Then I told Shyanna I had to take the special one straight to Rachel. Shy said she'd come with me.

Rachel's dad greeted us at the door and smiled when I gushed about the magical top. "You would make my wife proud," he said, smiling. "Rachel's in her room."

I wanted to surprise Rachel, so I lifted my finger to my lips to tell Shy to be quiet. We quietly swam around the corner to her room and spotted Rachel on her bed. She was lying down with her head on her pillow, and she was weeping as if her heart was breaking into two.

Shyanna and I stopped. Rachel must have sensed us because she looked up. She immediately sat up straight, sniffled, and wiped her tears away.

"Hello," she said, trying to sound cheerful. "What are you doing here? I think there's something in my eye."

"What's wrong, Rachel?" Shyanna asked.

We both swam to Rachel's bed and floated gently down next to her.

"What is it?" I asked.

"It's nothing. Nothing. Did everyone like the shell top?" she asked.

I crossed my arms. "You know they loved it. But we are not going to pretend that nothing is wrong. You're upset. And I think I know why."

Rachel's chin dropped, and she wouldn't look at Shyanna or me.

"It's Regina, isn't it?" I asked. "What has she done?"

"I don't want to ruin your happiness," Rachel said and her bottom lip quivered.

"We're best friends," I said. "If something is making you unhappy, we have to do something about it. After all, I certainly don't want to hear any more talk about you going off to live as a human again. That was just crazy."

"Tell us!" Shyanna insisted.

Rachel swallowed and looked at me. Then she lowered her eyes.

"Regina saw me watching the dress rehearsal," Rachel whispered. "She told me to leave. She told me half-humans couldn't represent a mermaid kingdom, and that she didn't want me to ruin her rehearsal."

My mouth dropped wide open. I glanced at Shyanna, who looked shocked too.

"Did she actually say that?" I asked.

Rachel nodded. She looked miserable.

"I'm leaving the special mermaid dance group," Shyanna said. "If that is how the leader is treating merpeople, I don't want any part of it."

"Me too," I said as my heart twisted. It hurt to think about not competing, but it wasn't worth all of this unhappiness.

"Happiness and friendship are what being a mermaid is all about," I reassured Rachel. "Not

58

nastiness or discrimination. Nobody should have to put up with that."

"You can't leave," Rachel insisted. "It's okay. I'm fine. Maybe I took it the wrong way. I'm just feeling sorry for myself. It doesn't mean you two should give up your dream."

Shyanna looked at me. We both knew it was more my dream than hers. But I shook my head.

"No. What Regina said is not okay. It's not okay. I can't believe the others feel this way too."

"Neither can I," Shyanna said.

I jumped up with a new determination. "I can't let this happen. I need to work this out."

"Cora?" Shy called and swam quickly after me.

"It's okay," I whispered to her. "You stay here with Rachel. She needs one of us. I'm going to have a special meeting with Cassie. If anyone can help with this, she can."

Shy nodded. "Okay," she said. "Good luck."

Chapter eight

I swam straight to Cassie's cave. She answered the door.

"Why didn't Rachel Marlin make it onto the special mermaid dance group?" I asked, not wasting any time.

Cassie glanced around the kitchen, looking really uncomfortable. "I suppose some of the other merkids didn't think she was good enough for the team?"

I pressed my lips tightly and spoke slowly, trying not to be too angry at Cassie. "Are you aware of how talented Rachel is?"

Cassie sat down across from me, wrapping her long blonde hair around her finger, and avoided looking at me. "I know. Trust me, I wanted to have her on the team. I was outvoted."

"By Regina?" I asked.

"I don't think I'm supposed to say," she said.

"Well," I said angrily, "tell me this. Is it because Rachel's mum was human?"

Cassie's cheeks turned bright red. "I don't know, Cora. She didn't exactly say that."

"What other reason could there be? She's got a great voice and a great attitude. Plus, she's a great mermaid," I said.

Cassie sighed and shrugged. "I think maybe you should talk to Regina," she said. "There's not much I can do." She blinked at me with wide eyes, and I saw the sympathy in them. As if she wanted to help.

"Could you arrange a meeting for the whole Special mermaid dance group straight away?" I asked. I wasn't going to let it go. I couldn't ignore it.

Cassie swam up. "Regina isn't going to be happy, but I'll see what I can do," she said.

* * *

Within an hour, Cassie had managed to get everyone over to her cave.

"I've called a special meeting," I said to everyone gathered in Cassie's kitchen.

Regina swam to my side. "I'm not sure why you're calling a special meeting when you're clearly not the team leader," she said.

Cassie swam to my other side. "Let her speak, Regina." She glanced out to the group. "Put your hand up if you want to hear what Cora has to say."

Shyanna's hand shot up first. Slowly, other hands went up in the air. It wasn't everyone, but it was enough for me to continue.

"I don't think I need to remind you that we are a team," I said. "The qualities we are trying to display are pride and joy for the Mermaid Kingdom."

The merkids around the kitchen nodded and a couple even whistled their approval.

"We're competing against the best singers and dancers and performers in the entire Mermaid Kingdom," I went on. "And we should have the most spirited merpeople representing us."

"We all know that, Cora," Regina said, rolling her eyes. "That's why we picked everyone here. And that's why I've been nagging you about your performance. We want to win."

"Exactly," I said. "And if we really want to win, we need Rachel Marlin on our team. She has one of the best voices in the entire kingdom, and she lives here in Neptunia. I'd like to know why she wasn't selected to be on our team in the first place."

The room was completely silent for a moment.

"Her voice isn't the problem," one of the mergirls blurted out. Everyone looked at her, and her cheeks went as red as lobster tails. She glanced at Regina with fear in her eyes.

"What exactly is the problem, then?" I asked, staring directly at Regina.

"Oh, come on." Regina rolled her eyes again. "She's — well, she's different."

"We're all different," Shyanna said. She swam to the front and floated close to me.

"Rachel is half-human," Regina said. "No one else is different like that."

"So Rachel really was excluded from the special mermaid dance group because she's half-human?" Shyanna asked.

No one was brave enough to say anything or stand up to Regina.

"Why does that even matter?" I asked.

I didn't want to believe Rachel had been right. But no one was denying it.

I looked around the room. "I'm so ashamed," I said. "This is no way to treat anyone."

"Well, if that's the way you feel..." Regina held out her hand and studied the glitter on her nails.

"That's exactly the way I feel," I said.

"Me too," Shy said. "Come on, Cora. Let's go."

We swam out of the cave together.

"I can't believe everyone in the squad feels this way. It's just not right," Shyanna said sadly as we swam away.

"I don't believe everyone does. We have to go to the Queen," I insisted. "We have to talk to her. This isn't right."

Chapter nine

Even though we arrived at the castle unannounced, the Queen agreed to see us as soon as we told her guard it was about the Neptunia dance group.

We told her the whole story. "And that's why we decided to come to you," Shy finished.

"Oh dear," said the Queen. "Rachel is such a lovely mergirl. And a beautiful singer too. You three did such a fantastic job at my concert and at the carnival. I did wonder why she wasn't selected to represent our castle. Her father must be upset."

"I don't think he knows yet," I told the Queen.

She tapped her finger on her chin, thinking.

"Well," she finally said. "I can't force the team to add Rachel." She smiled. "But there may be another solution." She paused for effect. "You could form a new group."

Shyanna and I looked at each other. "A new group?" I repeated.

The Queen nodded. "Each castle is allowed to enter more than one team. We've never done it before because we're one of the smaller castles. But..." She tilted her head slightly. "It can be done."

Shyanna and I smiled at each other. That just might work!

"We could recruit all the merkids in Neptunia who wanted to be on the special mermaid dance group, but who didn't make it or were afraid to audition because of Regina," Shyanna said.

I nodded in agreement. "We could do it!"

"It sounds like a good idea," the Queen said.

"A Special mermaid dance group that won't exclude anyone." She lifted a finger in the air. "I hereby appoint Cora Bass as the team leader for special mermaid dance group 2."

"This is amazing!" I squealed.

The Queen smiled and sat up straighter in her chair. "Okay, off with you two." She spoke in her more regal voice and lifted her chin. "You have work to do. And it's time for my diving lessons."

We swam up, thanking her for her time and her great idea. She waved her hand in the air and another mermaid appeared. We both immediately recognized her. The swimming teacher was the Sea Olympic Champion, Sydney Lincoln!

"Oh, and girls?" the Queen called as we swam down the Royal Hallway.

We both turned back.

"Make us proud!"

Shyanna and I swam away and didn't say another word until we were outside the castle. We both stopped at the same time, let out big breaths, and started to giggle uncontrollably.

Just as quickly as I started laughing, I stopped. "Oh my goodness." I put my hand on my chest. "What have we just agreed to? Can we do this in such a short amount of time?"

"I don't know," Shyanna said. "But we have to go and tell Rachel the news."

We swam as fast as we could back towards Rachel's cave. "We have some quick recruiting and lots of practising to do," I added as we raced to her cave. "And I have to call my mum and see if she'll even give me permission to do this."

"You know she will," Shyanna said.

"I don't know," I replied, suddenly worried. "My sisters are a handful, and she needs my help a lot."

"When she hears the whole story, she'll understand how important it is," Shyanna said.

* * *

When we got to Rachel's house, Mr Marlin answered the door. Shyanna spilled the news, including an exact recital of our conversation with the Queen.

"She's a brilliant Queen," he said, and then the grin on his face stretched wide. "And Rachel deserves to be on a special mermaid dance group!"

"Rachel!" we all shouted. "We have work to do!"

Rachel was thrilled about the new group. Her dad even offered to help us train once we'd got more people together.

Shy and I called our mothers, and as Shy predicted, my mum was more than happy to give me the night off from babysitting for emergency recruitment for the new special mermaid dance group. She said she'd manage without me as long as I needed to make my new group work. I heard the pride in her voice, and my heart swelled.

Shyanna's mum was happy too, and promised to make our entire group matching sea-shell headbands.

"By the way," Rachel said, "that top you borrowed isn't magic. The magic comes from believing in yourself. Your singing was all you."

"No way!" I said. "You are pretty sneaky, Rachel."

"Magic or not, we have lots of work to do," Shyanna said. "Let's get started!"

We sat down and came up with a list of everyone who had tried out for the special mermaid dance group but hadn't made it. We added a few names of merkids who we knew would love to be on the team, but were afraid of Regina.

Once we had finished our list, we swam through the entire castle, going door to door to personally ask the mermaids and merboys on our list if they wanted to join our group.

"It's going to be lots of work," we warned each of them. "We'll have to put in extra hours to be ready in time. We only have a few days."

Some mermaids and merboys didn't want to do it. But many did. By the end of the night, we had an enthusiastic and complete team. As team leader, I had to work out what to do with them in a very short time.

It was up to me. I wondered if I could handle it.

Chapter ten

Regina laughed when we told her we were resigning from her team and starting a new special mermaid dance group.

"I have the entire sports hall booked," she said with a toss of her hair. "I can't afford to share it. You'll have to find somewhere else to rehearse."

"No problem." Rachel smirked. "We don't need it."

The team agreed to meet at Walrus Waterpark after school to practise. Our first rehearsal proved we had a team with a lot of heart and oodles of spirit. Everyone was focused and willing to work hard to learn a routine in a short time. The only trouble was, I couldn't get everyone to agree to sing the song I'd chosen. I knew it was a hard song, but it was one of my favourites.

Instead of wasting time arguing about it, we agreed to work on the dance routine while we thought about the song.

I showed everyone the choreography I'd come up with. Together we adjusted the moves to fit the skills and limitations of our team members. We all worked together, improvising and improving the moves.

The results were astonishing. It was obvious the dance routine was going to be our biggest strength as a team. All the merkids worked together. Our willingness to help each other shine and show off our differences was a definite advantage. We left our first rehearsal with a solid routine that everyone loved.

Shyanna, Rachel and I left together. As soon as we were out of the park, I burst into tears.

"Cora? What's wrong?" Shyanna asked.

"I'm happy, tired and a little bit stressed," I said as I cried like a little baby. "I can't even get everyone to agree on a song, and we only have three days left to learn everything."

Rachel swam in front of me. "Don't be silly, Cora. You put together the most amazing routine I've ever seen. You've managed to get everyone to take ownership and work together. You were brilliant."

"I'd like to help," a soft voice said.

I sniffled and looked up. It was Cassie Shore.

"I've left the Neptunia special mermaid dance group." She looked at Rachel. "I knew it was wrong – the reason you didn't make it onto the team. I'm sorry I didn't stick up for you sooner. I think it's fantastic that you're half-human."

"It's okay," Rachel said quietly.

Cassie nodded. "I'm on your side."

Rachel smiled. "There shouldn't be any sides. We're all merpeople."

Cassie turned to me. "I saw you practising, and I couldn't help noticing that you were having trouble with your song. I would love to help."

"Oh, yes! You're a songwriter!" I shouted.

Cassie nodded.

"On one condition," I said. "I think our group will do better if Rachel is our team leader. Can you work with her to rewrite the song and help her teach it to the rest of the group?"

Rachel gasped. "Really, Cora? You want me to be team leader?"

"You're the best singer," I said. I glanced at Shyanna. "Well, you and Shy."

Shy laughed. "It's okay. Rachel is good. And she's much better at performing than I am. It's a great choice, Cora!"

The four of us put our hands out and piled them on top of one another in a perfect team huddle.

"We still have lots of work to do," I said. "But I'm glad we're all doing it together."

Chapter eleven

"Mermen and mermaids, merboys and mergirls, welcome to the Mermaid Kingdom Festival to celebrate our one-hundredth anniversary," announced the King of Caspian Castle. "First to compete, from Neptunia Castle, special mermaid dance group 2!"

The crowd cheered. I glanced at Shyanna. She looked like she was about to be sick. Stage fright was a big thing for her.

"It's okay, Shy. You're far from alone. And you always do fantastically," I whispered.

She nodded, took a big breath, and swam out into the giant field we would be performing in. From the opposite end of the field, Rachel swam to meet her in the middle. As rehearsed, we were all quiet and still, and then the two of them opened their mouths and started to sing.

The rest of the team swam in fast, doing flips over each other like a giant game of leapfrog. Then Rachel rolled out a big ball of glowing plankton that exploded like fireworks. The effects were amazing, and the crowd roared with approval.

The whole team started singing the song that Cassie had composed and Rachel had taught us, and we moved together in a giant wave of motion. We had even added special effects to our routine by using lots of glowing creatures.

There were a few mistakes in our performance here and there, but the crowd was cheering so loudly that I don't think anyone noticed the glitches. I could not believe it was happening.

The finale came quickly, and we all worked together and jumped and sprang off each other like we had rehearsed. The final roar of our team could be heard throughout the entire kingdom. "Neptunia!" we shouted as one.

After the crowd settled down, the swimming gala got underway. There would be a few more events, and then the other dance groups would perform their routines. I was really looking forward to seeing what the other groups had put together.

Our team huddled together once we swam off of the field. "I'm so proud of every single one of you!" Rachel said. "No matter what happens!"

Merpeople from every castle flocked over to congratulate us. Regina swam by, her nose in the air. "I noticed so many errors in that first performance. How embarrassing," she said to her new co-captain, loud enough for us to hear.

"Yeah, but the performance was pretty spectacular," the co-captain said. "All those special effects and moves were ambitious for a group that have only just got together. And those mermaids can really sing!"

Rachel giggled. "She won't be co-captain for long," she whispered to me.

Our entire team was sitting together when they announced the winner. It was the team from Hercules Castle. Their routine had been the best.

Shyanna swam over to us then. "Rachel! Guess who's arrived to surprise you? He was in the crowd and saw our performance."

"Owen's here?" Rachel asked, grinning.

"He didn't know what time we performed so he got here early. He's only got his tail for another hour, so come on." Shy grabbed Rachel's arm. "Come on, Cora!" she shouted to me.

"I'll be there in a minute. I have to find my family!" I called and waved them off.

Everyone around me had disappeared. I closed my eyes and took a deep breath to enjoy the moment.

The pace had been crazy over the last few days, but it had been worth it. Our performance was over, and we'd done really well.

When I opened my eyes, my mum was swimming towards me. She was alone, which hardly ever happened. "Where are the girls?" I asked.

She smiled. "Your sisters are with your father. He needs some practise handling all of them at once. He took some time off of work so I could come and see you." She winked and floated to my side. "That was an amazing show!"

I put my head on her shoulder, enjoying having her all to myself. "Thanks, Mum. I wanted to make you proud. We didn't win, but that's okay. We have lots of heart, but other teams had more time to train. There are a lot of other competitions left."

Mum put a finger under my chin and looked right into my eyes. "You stuck up for your friend. You made difficult choices, and you did the right thing. Like you always do. You make me prouder than you

can ever imagine!" She softly hummed the song we'd sung. "You're the best daughter and the best big sister a family could have."

"Thanks, Mum," I said, giving her the biggest hug I could.

"I love you, Cora," she said.

As we swam away, I couldn't stop smiling.

Legend of mermaids

These creatures of the sea have many secrets. Although people have believed in mermaids for centuries, nobody has ever proven their existence. People all over the world are attracted to mysterious mermaids.

The earliest mermaid story dates back to around 1000 BC in an Assyrian legend. A goddess loved a human man but killed him accidentally. She fled to the water in shame. She tried to change into a fish, but the water would not let her hide her true nature. She lived the rest of her days as half-woman, half-fish.

Later, the ancient Greeks whispered tales of fishy women called sirens. These beautiful but deadly beings lured sailors to their graves. Many sailors feared or respected mermaids because of their association with doom.

Note: This text was taken from *The Girl's Guide to Mermaids: Everything Alluring about These Mythical Beauties* by Sheri A. Johnson (Capstone Press, 2012).

Talk about it

1. Cora had always dreamed about being on the special mermaid dance group. However, it didn't quite work out how she thought it would. Describe a time when your expectations had to change.

2. When Cora and Shyanna found out why Rachel didn't make it onto the special mermaid dance group, they were rightfully upset. Do you think they did the right thing when they talked to the Queen? What would you have done in the same situation?

3. Rachel didn't want her friends to find out how she really felt. Why is it important to talk about your feelings?

4. With three little sisters, Cora had a lot of extra responsibilities at home. Did you think it was fair that she had to help out so much? Defend your answer.

Write it down

1. Pretend you're Cora. Write a "for" and "against" list of reasons for leaving the dance group.

2. If Cora and Shyanna hadn't left the special mermaid dance group for Rachel, do you think the three girls would still be friends? Write a few paragraphs explaining your answer.

3. In this story, Regina was the nasty girl/bully. Why do you think Regina acted like this? Write a few paragraphs from Regina's point of view. Make sure you include reasons for her actions, as they will help readers understand Regina better.

4. Write an alternate ending to the story. Perhaps the two dance groups from Neptunia tie and have to compete against each other. Perhaps the two dance groups form one big squad and compete together? It's your ending, so you can finish the story in whatever way you think best.

About the author

Janet Gurtler has written many well-received books for the Young Adult market. Mermaid Kingdom is her first series for younger readers. She lives near the Canadian Rockies in Calgary, Canada, with her husband, son and a chubby Chihuahua called Bruce.

About the illustrator

Katie Wood fell in love with drawing
when she was very young. Since graduating
from Loughborough University School
of Art and Design in 2004, she has been
living her dream working as a freelance
illustrator. From her studio in Leicester,
she creates bright and lively illustrations for
books and magazines all over the world.